CHANCE'S LUCKY DAY

STORY BY: LAURIE GIFFORD ADAMS

ILLUSTRATED BY: NISSA BURCH

CHANCE'S LUCKY DAY

Chance stared at the door in the animal shelter. The workers there took good care of him and the other animals, but this wasn't a forever home. Like the other dogs, he had been waiting a long time for a family of his own. Would today finally be his lucky day when someone would take him home?

The big door opened. The bright lights snapped on. Some of the dogs barked, but Chance was quiet. A woman walked in with Kim, the worker who feeds Chance and the other dogs.

Chance sat up, lifted his ears, and smiled with his tongue hanging out. His wagging tail swish-swished on the floor. He wanted the woman to know he was friendly.

"This puppy is Chance," Kim said.
"Maybe you would like to adopt him."

The woman stopped and looked,
but then she shook her head.

"No, I can't get a puppy," she said. "I need an older dog who will sit with my grandfather to keep him company."

The woman passed by Chance. He watched her stop and look at the dogs in other cages. A few minutes later she walked by with a golden dog on a leash. It was Belle. Her eyes sparkled with happiness. Chance hoped someday he would look that happy, too.

Later, Kim brought in a man, woman, and little girl. The girl skipped toward Chance's cage. It made him so happy that he ran back and forth in front of her with his tail wagging.

"Daddy, look at this cute puppy. Can we adopt him?" the girl asked.

Her dad shook his head. "We have a very small yard," he said. "That puppy would need a place where he can run. He wouldn't be happy at our house."

Kim pointed to the brown and white dog in the next cage.

"What about Oreo?" she asked. "She likes to stay indoors and is happy to sit on laps."

The mom nodded and said, "Oreo is the right dog for us! We'll adopt her."

Chance watched them put a blue leash on Oreo. She pranced next to the little girl as they left.

Chance was happy Oreo was getting her forever home. When the door clicked shut behind them, he couldn't stop wondering when his lucky day would come. He wouldn't give up hope. Tomorrow was a new day and a new chance.

That night, he curled up on his sleeping mat. Chance imagined what it would be like to have a family. What would they do together? Would they go for rides? Would they snuggle? Would they brush his fur? Would he have toys? Where would he sleep?

He closed his eyes and dreamed about the life he hoped he would have. His new home would be perfect.

The next day, three more families came in. Chance always sat and behaved his best. Each time the people looked toward Chance's cage, but they didn't stop. He wasn't the right dog for them.

When they left, Kim took Chance out to play in the fenced yard. She threw an orange ball and Chance chased it. He jumped and jumped and ran in circles.

"Chance, let's sit on the grass," Kim said. She patted a spot next to her. Chance dashed over because he knew Kim would pet him. It was nice, but it wasn't the same as having his own family who would pet him every day.

"Don't give up, Chance," Kim said. "Good things come to those who wait. When the perfect family for you comes in, you'll feel it."

The next morning, Chance was eating his breakfast when he heard something he liked. His ears popped up to listen. It was a man on the other side of the door who sounded happy and fun.

Something in Chance's heart tingled.
This man sounded like someone Chance would like.

When the door opened, Kim came in with a tall man wearing a blue baseball cap. Chance grabbed the orange ball Kim had given him and carried it to the cage door. He wanted the man to think he was fun, too.

"I think I have the perfect dog for you," Kim said. She and the tall man walked right toward Chance's cage.

Chance's tail whipped the air. They were talking about *him*!

"Chance, would you like to meet Ed?" Kim asked.

She opened the door, and Chance stepped out of his cage. He dropped the ball in front of Ed, and it bounced by his feet.

Ed picked up the ball and kneeled next to Chance. He looked right into Chance's eyes.

"Hello, Chance. Our old dog was my children's best friend. They miss him very much. I want to surprise them with a new best friend. Do you know any puppies who are looking for best friends?"

Chance wagged his tail. Yes! Yes! He wanted best friends!

"You would live on a farm where you can play with children and have lots of room to run," Ed said.

Chance panted and smiled big. His tail wagged so hard that his whole body swayed. This was exactly what he had been dreaming about.

Ed looked at Kim. "I think Chance will be
the perfect dog for my family."

Chance was so excited that he jumped around Ed and Kim.

"I have a brand-new collar for you. Can you sit, Chance?" Ed asked.

Chance sat and tried not to wiggle. Ed looped a bright yellow collar
around Chance's neck, then snapped on a matching leash.

"Let's go home," Ed said.

Home. It was the best word Chance had ever heard.

When Ed put his face closer, Chance licked his cheek. Ed laughed
the same way he had when Chance first heard him. Kim was right.
He could feel in his heart that he had found his family.

The other dogs in cages stared at Chance. He barked once to tell
them not to give up hope. One day, their person
would walk through that door, too.

Chance proudly trotted as they went out to Ed's red truck. Ed picked him up and put him in the back seat. He clicked Chance's leash into the seatbelt so he'd be safe and closed the door.

Chance couldn't believe this was really happening. It was hard for him to sit still because he was so excited. His dream was coming true. He was getting a family and a home!

A cool breeze blew through the open window and ruffled Chance's fur. He lifted his nose to sniff. The air smelled different.

Today the air smelled like love.

At the farm, Ed helped Chance out of the truck.

A woman waved from the porch of a pretty, white farmhouse.

Behind the house was a red barn. There were different animals in
the pasture next to it. Chance tipped his head and stared.
They were the biggest, funniest-looking dogs he had ever seen.

His new home looked very exciting. He couldn't wait to explore.

"Risa! Noah! Come outside. There's a surprise for you,"
the woman called.

Suddenly, the door behind the woman banged open and a boy and girl burst from the house.

"A puppy!" Noah cried as he raced across the grass.

"Is he ours?" Risa asked, chasing close behind.

Ed unsnapped the leash, and Chance ran to the children.

"Yes. His name is Chance, and he's all ours."

The children dropped to their knees on the lawn and wrapped their arms around Chance. He squirmed so he could lick their faces.

Risa giggled and Noah laughed. At the same time, Chance felt the tingle in his heart just like Kim said. He knew that Risa and Noah would be his best friends.

"Welcome home, Chance!" Risa said. She gave him a kiss on his head. "We can't wait for our adventures together."

"We're going to love you forever," Noah whispered in Chance's ear.

A warm feeling raced through Chance's whole body. He wedged himself between Noah and Risa and licked their cheeks again. He knew for sure he finally had a family of his own.

Today was Chance's lucky day.

ABOUT THE AUTHOR

Laurie Gifford Adams is the author of books in many genres. She's excited to break the conventions of children's picture books by combining the fun of illustrations with narrative that tells a richer story.

Learn more about the author at www.lauriegiffordadams.com or follow her on Facebook at Laurie Gifford Adams - Author.

ABOUT THE ILLUSTRATOR

Nissa Burch is a psychology student at Purdue University Global. She is excited to be illustrating a second children's book. (Her first illustration foray was in the best-selling middle grades novel *Pawprints in the Snow*, also written by Laurie Gifford Adams.) Nissa's passion for drawing began in sixth grade, and in the near future, her goal is to become an art therapist.

You can see more of her work at https://nissaburch.wixsite.com/website

CPSIA information can be obtained
at www.ICGtesting.com
Printed in the USA
BVHW021157221122
652529BV00002B/18